Pioneers of Light and Sound

by Connie Jankowski

Science Contributor
Sally Ride Science
Science Consultant
Michael E. Kopecky, Science Educator
Jane Weir, Physicist

MISSION: SCIENCE

Developed with contributions from Sally Ride Science™

Sally Ride
Science

Sally Ride Science™ is an innovative content company dedicated to fueling young people's interests in science.

Our publications and programs provide opportunities for students and teachers to explore the captivating world of science—from astrobiology to zoology.

We bring science to life and show young people that science is creative, collaborative, fascinating, and fun.

To learn more, visit www.SallyRideScience.com

First hardcover edition published in 2010 by
Compass Point Books
151 Good Counsel Drive
P.O. Box 669
Mankato, MN 56002-0669

Editor: Mari Bolte
Designer: Heidi Thompson
Editorial Contributor: J. M. Bedell
Media Researcher: Svetlana Zhurkin
Production Specialist: Jane Klenk

 This book was manufactured with paper containing at least 10 percent post-consumer waste.

Library of Congress Cataloging-in-Publication Data
Jankowski, Connie.
  Pioneers of light and sound / by Connie Jankowski.—1st hardcover ed.
    p. cm.—(Mission. Science)
  Includes index.
  ISBN 978-0-7565-4306-8 (library binding)
  1. Optics—Juvenile literature. 2. Sound—Juvenile literature.
3. Optical instruments—Juvenile literature. 4. Electronic apparatus and
appliances—Juvenile literature. 5. Discoveries in science—Juvenile
literature. I. Title. II. Series.
  QC360.J365 2009
  535.09—dc22   2009029360

Visit Compass Point Books, a Capstone imprint, on the Internet at *www.compasspointbooks.com*
or e-mail your request to *custserv@compasspointbooks.com*

Table of Contents

Scientists estimate that the universe is billions of years old. As the universe developed, galaxies formed, and within each galaxy, planets, moons, and stars appeared. There are more than 100 billion galaxies in the universe. At the edge of the Milky Way galaxy is a star called the sun.

The sun is not the largest or the smallest star in the universe. But the sun is important, because it gives Earth heat and light. Without heat and light, all living things on Earth would die.

Around the sun orbit eight planets, their moons, and Pluto, which is a planetoid. Earth is the perfect distance from the sun to support life—not so close that everything burns, but not so far away that everything freezes.

Scientists don't know when light first appeared, but it probably happened while the very first star was being formed. Sound probably came along when

Did You Know?

Our solar system is predicted to be around 4.5 billion years old. Rocks as old as 3.8 billion years have been found all over Earth.

The Milky Way

Ancient Greek astronomers gazed into the night sky and saw what looked like a river of milk around Earth. They called it *galactos*, which means milk. Galactos is also the source of the word *galaxy*. In Latin, Milky Way is *Via Lactea*. *Via* means way or road, and *lactea* means milk—the milky road.

Later the scientist Galileo Galilei looked through his telescope and discovered that the milky road was actually thousands of individual stars. Hundreds of years after Galilei's discovery, scientists realized that those stars were only the edge of an entire galaxy.

the first planet developed an atmosphere, because sound can't exist without an atmosphere to move through.

Throughout the centuries, scientists have been fascinated with light and sound. Long ago they learned that light waves are the movement of electromagnetic energy. They found out that sound waves were caused by moving atoms. They also discovered that light and sound waves can be managed and used to improve everyday life. Here are some of the scientists who dedicated their lives to understanding light and sound.

There are between 200 billion and 400 billion stars in the Milky Way.

While Western Europe was slogging through the Dark Ages, the people of the Middle East were entering a golden age of science. Many Arab scientists conducted groundbreaking experiments in astronomy, chemistry, medicine, philosophy, and physics. The greatest scientists was Al-Hassan Ibn al-Haytham.

Haytham was born in Basra, Iraq, and was educated in Baghdad. His most important writings were about light. His seven-volume work titled *The Book of Optics* is often considered the most influential book in the history of physics. At a time when many people thought a beam of light coming from the eye allowed sight, Haytham's work proved that sight actually happened when light entered the eye.

Haytham realized that light had a limited speed and traveled in a straight line. He invented the artificial lens, and experimented

Al-Hassan Ibn al-Haytham has been called the father of optics.

with the reflection and refraction of light. His work laid the foundation for the invention of the telescope and the microscope. He also described the pinhole camera, and invented the camera obscura, which eventually led to the modern camera.

By the end of his life, Haytham had written more than 200 books. None of his original Arabic language works survived, but 65 Latin translations still exist.

Isaac Newton was born in England at the height of the scientific revolution. By the end of the 1700s, science had replaced religion as the strongest force in European society.

Newton attended Trinity College in Cambridge, where he studied physics and mathematics. He became the leading mathematician in Europe. But when he graduated in 1665, few people knew about his work, and his genius went unnoticed by the university.

That same year, the plague forced the college to close. Newton spent two years at home. He studied the works of earlier scientists, including Francesco Grimaldi's work with optics.

When Trinity College reopened, Newton was elected to a fellowship. Later he became a professor of mathematics.

Isaac Newton was one of the greatest scientists and mathematicians of all time.

As a professor, he was freed from the demands of tutoring students, but he had to lecture on his work. He chose to lecture on optics, while continuing his experiments with light.

Newton's experiments changed the way people thought about light. He

Francesco Grimaldi (1618—1663)

Francesco Grimaldi was one of the first scientists to suggest that light traveled in waves. He also discovered that light breaks apart in a process he called diffraction.

argued that light was made of tiny particles that could be broken down into individual rays. He said each ray's color depended on the size of its particles. Red light particles were the largest, then green, and then blue. Newton called this phenomenon inflection, but Grimaldi's word for it, diffraction, is still used today.

Newton also said that each light ray refracts— it changes direction. The angle of refraction determines the color that is seen. Refracted light caused problems for people trying to use the first telescopes. Light passing through a lens distorted the image, and it had strange colors around its edges. To solve these problems, Newton invented the refracting telescope, which lets modern astronomers use very large lenses to see distant images clearly.

Newton's book *Principia*, published in 1687, established him as one of England's greatest thinkers.

A later English scientist, Thomas Young, believed that the structure of the eye allowed people to see. He suggested that the eye sees color because of three nerve fibers in the retina. One responds to red, one to green, and one to violet light.

At that time, people believed Newton's theory that light was made of particles called corpuscles. Young experimented with a beam of light passing through two slits in a thick card and shining onto a wall. If light was made of corpuscles, it should appear normal on the wall, but it didn't. Instead, some parts were bright and others dark, suggesting that light is a wave. He also proposed that the color of light depends on its wavelength, the distance between the peaks of two waves.

Augustin Fresnel, a civil engineer, confirmed Young's work. He wrote the laws of the diffraction of light, which showed how diffraction patterns could be predicted.

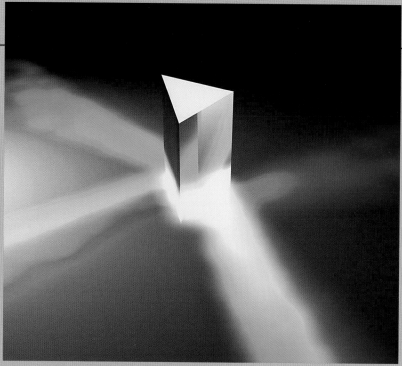

When light passes through glass or other transparent objects, the light waves slow and bend. Each wave bends at a slightly different angle, separating it from the others and creating a rainbow.

Elsa Garmire
(1939–   )

Elsa Garmire is an expert with lasers and has nine patents for laser-related inventions. She was the first person to create a laser light show for an audience. One of her inventions is even earning money—it uses lasers to remove graffiti from public places.

Louis-Jacques-Mandé Daguerre was a French artist and chemist. He worked as a stage designer in Paris and became famous in the 1820s for his dioramas—works of art made with giant paintings. By lighting the paintings carefully, Daguerre could make a scene change from night to day, from winter to summer. He could make things appear and disappear. Daguerre added real objects, creating scenes that looked as though a person could walk right into them.

While trying to improve his dioramas, Daguerre discovered a way to capture an image on paper by using light and chemicals. He had invented the world's first successful photo. He called the new process a daguerreotype. Because it shortened the time people needed to sit for a photograph to 30 minutes, it became popular for taking portraits. Earlier photographs had faded quickly, but the daguerreotype process made images that could last for decades.

Daguerreotypes were delicate, hard to see from some angles, and impossible to reproduce. But they were exciting,

Patience, Please

People who posed for daguerrotypes had to sit still for as long as half an hour. If they moved, the picture would be blurry. That's why people in early photographs are not smiling. They couldn't hold a smile in place that long!

Daguerreotypes taken of cities did not show any people. This was because people moved too fast for the camera to capture, making any moving objects "invisible."

because for the first time people could see, and even own, images of reality. Daguerre's photographic method is still valued today. Examples of this style are preserved in museums and private collections.

Daguerre's artistic eye and scientific curiosity combined to give the world a gift. His work began the era of photography, which changed the way people think about the world.

Oberlin Smith had a curious mind. He liked to tinker with objects that he thought he could improve. Sound and picture recording, computer hard drives, and garage door openers came from Smith's ideas. He held more than 70 patents during his lifetime.

Smith was born in Cincinnati, Ohio. He attended the Philadelphia Polytechnic Institute where he studied drafting, blacksmithing, and other skills needed for manufacturing products. After college, he started a metalworking and die and press design company. His company was responsible for the technology needed to stamp out fenders for bicycles and cars from sheets of steel.

Smith associated with other inventors of his day including Alexander Graham Bell and Thomas Edison. After seeing Edison's phonograph, Smith experimented with various ways of capturing sound. Instead of Edison's grooves etched in tinfoil, he used a string made of cotton or silk with tiny pieces of wire embedded into it. Sound was recorded when the wire was magnetized.

Like most of his work, Smith never patented his magnetic recorder. He documented his work by drawing a diagram, writing a description, putting the papers in a sealed envelope, and filing them with the county clerk. No one knows if he ever built

15

a recorder because many of his records were accidentally destroyed. In 1888 Smith placed his magnetic recording idea into the public domain by publishing it in the engineering magazine, *Electrical World*.

Smith invented other devices that are familiar. For example, he built a record changer and a remote control so he could sit in his chair and listen to records stored in a cupboard in another room. Smith was considered one of the greatest mechanical engineers of his generation.

Oberlin Smith's record changer was an early relative of the jukebox.

Lawrence J. Fogel (1928—2007)

Lawrence J. Fogel patented the first noise canceling system. It is used in helicopter and airplane cockpits. Noise cancellation uses sound waves of the same amplitude as the noise to be blocked, but inverts the wave. When the two sound waves meet, the inversion cause the waves to cancel each other out.

Alexander Graham Bell (1847–1922)

Can you imagine life without telephones? Many people depend on phones to run their businesses, do their jobs, and keep in touch with friends and family.

Alexander Graham Bell filed the first patent for the telephone. Many other people invented similar machines about the same time, but Bell's design beat all the others. He made a fortune from his invention.

Bell was born in Scotland. He was educated at home and then attended Edinburgh's Royal High School. His first job was teaching music and diction to children, and by age 20, he was a resident master in Elgin's Weston House Academy. While at the academy, he started his work in the study of sound.

Following the deaths of his two brothers, Bell and his

Bell speaking into an early model telephone

parents moved to Canada. In 1871 he went to the United States to lecture on teaching speech to the deaf and to open a school for teachers of the deaf in Boston.

Bell was an intelligent man, but not good with his hands. So when he met Thomas Watson, a repair mechanic and model maker, he asked him to help with his experiments. Watson agreed. Night after night, the two men searched for ways to transmit sound using electricity, and to build a working transmission device.

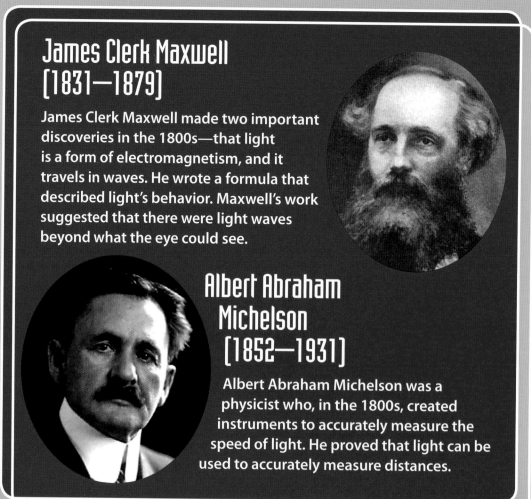

James Clerk Maxwell (1831—1879)

James Clerk Maxwell made two important discoveries in the 1800s—that light is a form of electromagnetism, and it travels in waves. He wrote a formula that described light's behavior. Maxwell's work suggested that there were light waves beyond what the eye could see.

Albert Abraham Michelson (1852—1931)

Albert Abraham Michelson was a physicist who, in the 1800s, created instruments to accurately measure the speed of light. He proved that light can be used to accurately measure distances.

Bell and Watson were eventually successful. Their device could translate the vibrations of sound into electrical current and send it along a wire. At the other end, a similar device converted the current back into sound vibrations. They had invented the telephone.

Did You Know?

Bell invented the metal detector. One of its earliest uses was to find an assassin's bullet in President James Garfield's body. But the detector went off no matter what part of Garfield's body it was pointed at. Later people realized that the bed Garfield was laying on had metal springs that set off the alarm.

Bell speaking into his telephone

Sound Waves and Science

Sound waves are used to see 3-D images of the inside of the human body, to destroy tumors, kidney stones, and gallstones without making an incision, and to treat cancer, strokes, and Parkinson's disease. They are also used to control bleeding, to deliver drugs, and to kill bacteria.

Tom Brown, Ian Donald, and John MacVicar invented the first ultrasound machine. They realized that sonar technology could be used to look inside the human body. They unveiled their invention in 1958.

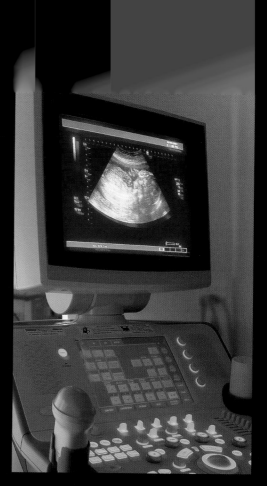

In 1876 they made the first long distance telephone call. Their conversation was transmitted over a wire that stretched two miles (3.2 kilometers), from Cambridge to Boston, Massachusetts. That same year, at the Centennial Expo in Philadelphia, Bell unveiled his new telephone. He was granted a U.S. patent and within months was swamped with lawsuits challenging his claim. Although he became embroiled in the most complicated patent litigation in history, his patent rights were upheld.

As a young boy, Thomas Edison loved to study new things. He liked to read, but he didn't speak until he was 4 years old. His teachers didn't think he would amount to much. His mother took him out of school and helped him learn at home.

When Edison was a teen, he left home and traveled around the United States. He found work as a telegraph operator. The telegraph used electric signals sent through wires to send messages. This gave Edison the idea of using electricity in other ways.

In 1879 he made the first long-lasting lightbulb. He also invented a generator that could bring electricity to homes and businesses, making it possible to enjoy his lightbulbs.

Edison also studied sound. In 1877 he invented the phonograph, a machine that could play back recorded sounds. He first tested his machine by recording "Mary Had a Little Lamb" and was astonished when the machine repeated his words back to him.

Visitors can see Edison's laboratory in West Orange, New Jersey.

In 1903 Edison introduced people to the first "talking picture." Only 12 minutes long, *The Great Train Robbery*'s 14 scenes blended moving pictures with sound. It was the first narrated motion picture.

At the time of his death, Edison held more than 1,000 patents—many of which involved light and sound.

Thomas Edison speaking into his phonograph

Victoria Cerami [1960—   ]

Victoria Cerami is an expert in acoustical engineering—the science of designing buildings that allow sound to carry well within them. She first learned about acoustics from her father, who was also an engineer and acoustics expert.

Today Cerami's company does acoustic work around the world, from IMAX theaters to courtrooms. She says that courtrooms are especially tough to work with. Judges and lawyers need to speak privately, and Cerami must figure out how to make that possible.

Did You Know?

The final scene of *The Great Train Robbery* depicts a bandit shooting directly at the camera. Many audience members thought they were actually about to be shot.

George Eastman (1854-1932)

George Eastman was an American businessman and inventor. By 1880 he had invented a way to develop film using a dry formula and a machine that could prepare many photographic plates at a time. He recognized the potential of his work and said, "We were starting out to make photography an everyday affair … [and] to make the camera as convenient as the pencil." Eastman trademarked the name Kodak in 1888 and founded the Eastman Kodak company in 1892.

To bring his inventions to the public, Eastman introduced his Kodak camera and film at world expositions. Year after year, he improved on the film processing and on the camera's design. By 1896 he had sold 100,000 cameras, and was manufacturing film at a rate of 400 miles (644 km) a month. Still not content, in 1900 he

Did You Know?

George Eastman created his famous brand name by arranging some of his favorite letters to form a word: Kodak.

introduced the Brownie, the first of many cameras to carry the name. The cameras were easy to use and cost a dollar each.

The Eastman Kodak Company kept growing and expanded its film technology into areas such as X-ray images, motion picture film, and copy machines. Today it is the largest supplier of photographic film in the world and also competes in the digital, photo processing, and motion picture industries.

▲ early camera

Kristina Johnson [1958—]

Kristina Johnson is a scientist who works with light. She is a leader in the field of optoelectronics, which combines light with electronics. She has worked with 3-D imaging and has discovered new ways to create miniature lights for displays and computer monitors.

Albert Einstein (1879-1955)

Albert Einstein is known as one of the greatest scientists of all time. Born in Ulm, Württemberg, Germany, young Albert didn't speak much and was a poor student. Some people thought he wasn't very smart.

In 1898 he attended the Swiss Federal Polytechnic School in Zurich, Switzerland, where he trained to be a physics and mathematics teacher. When he couldn't find a teaching position, he took a job at the Swiss patent office, where he specialized in electromagnetic devices.

Einstein spent his free time doing research and working on his first famous special theory of relativity. His first paper was published in the physics journal *Annalen der Physik* in 1905. In it he said the velocity of light—its speed and direction—never changes, even if the source of the light is moving. He also said no physical object could reach that velocity.

The speed of light is roughly 186,000 miles (300,000 km) per second.

In a second paper, a few months later, he wrote that an object's energy is equal to its mass (the amount of matter it contains). The paper presented one of the most famous equations in science: $E=mc^2$. E stands for energy, m means mass, and c^2 means the speed of light (c)

25

Lene Vestergaard Hau (1959—   )

Light's normal speed is 186,282 miles (299,792 km) per second, but a professor of physics at Harvard University, Lene Vestergaard Hau, has made it travel only 38 miles (61 km) per hour. For just a moment, in fact, she did what seemed impossible: She made light stand still.

How did Hau do it? She and her team of scientists made some tiny particles called atoms extremely cold. When light passed through the atoms, the light's speed dropped to about two-thirds of a mile (1 km) per second. Eventually they managed to make a pulse of light start, stop, and start again.

multiplied by itself. Einstein's equation meant that even a very small piece of matter could potentially release a huge amount of energy.

Did You Know?

Much to his dismay, Einstein saw his $E=mc^2$ equation come to life in August 1945. Atomic bombs were dropped on the Japanese cities of Hiroshima and Nagasaki, killing more than 220,000 people.

This equation changed science in many ways. It shows why nuclear energy can be so powerful, whether it is used to generate electricity or to build nuclear weapons. The fact that mass can be changed to energy also explains why the sun is so hot. Einstein's ideas were so new, and so impressive, that it's easy to see why he became world-famous.

In 1916 Einstein announced his general theory of relativity. He predicted that because of the sun's powerful gravity, rays of light coming from a distant star would bend as they passed the sun. Such bending was observed a few years later.

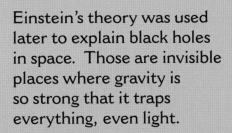

Einstein's theory was used later to explain black holes in space. Those are invisible places where gravity is so strong that it traps everything, even light.

Some scientists were skeptical of Einstein's ideas. Others just thought his work wasn't important or was too controversial. But in 1921, Einstein's work was finally recognized and he was awarded the Nobel Prize in physics.

Einstein spent the rest of his life teaching or doing research. In 1933 as the Nazi Party was gaining control of the German government, Einstein moved to the United States, becoming a citizen seven years later. He accepted a position as professor of theoretical physics at Princeton University and remained in Princeton, New Jersey, until his death in 1955.

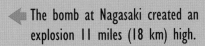
The bomb at Nagasaki created an explosion 11 miles (18 km) high.

Chemical Engineer: Jan Talbot

University of California, San Diego

In college Jan Talbot's hardest subject was chemistry. Instead of letting it defeat her, she decided to make it her focus.

There were hundreds of students in her chemistry classes. Sometimes she was the only woman. When the professor would say, "Good morning, gentlemen," she would wave her hand to remind him she was there, too.

Chemists can build and experiment with models of molecules on the computer

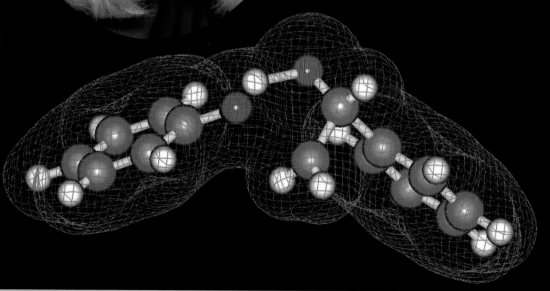

Talbot says she never got discouraged. "When you care about something, you don't listen to people who say you can't," she says. Being positive has paid off. Today she is a professor of nanoengineering—the creation of submicroscopic structures.

Did You Know?

A nanometer is one-billionth of a meter. Nanoengineering usually involves things on the scale of 1 to 100 nanometers.

Experts Tell Us ...

Why is Talbot a chemical engineer instead of a chemist? A chemist might study the reaction between two chemicals. A chemical engineer would figure out if the reaction solves any problems in the real world. "I like chemistry, but I really want to know how to use it to make something."

Think About It

Have people ever told you that you couldn't do something? What did you do about it?

Talbot enjoys a challenge such as a hike in the desert.

Lives and Work at a Glance

Al-Hassan Ibn al-Haytham

Fields of study: *Physics, mathematics*

Known for: *Writing* The Book of Optics

Known as: *Father of optics*

Nationality: *Arab*

Birthplace: *Basra, Iraq*

Date of birth: *965*

Date of death: *1038*

Awards and honors: *Has been called the first scientist*

Victoria Cerami

Field of study: *Acoustical engineering*

Known for: *Managing an internationally recognized acoustics consulting firm*

Nationality: *American*

Year of birth: *1960*

Awards and honors: *Galaxy Award, given by the New York Women's Agenda, 2001; Fairway To Life Progress Award, 2005*

Louis-Jacques-Mandé Daguerre

Fields of study: *Physics, chemistry*

Known for: *Inventing the diorama and the daguerreotype*

Nationality: *French*

Birthplace: *Paris, France*

Date of birth: *November 18, 1787*

Date of death: *July 10, 1851*

Awards and honors: *Council medal from the Great Exhibition, 1851; fellow of the Royal Society, 1853; photographer to the queen, 1858; chevalier of the Legion of Honour, 1863*

George Eastman

Field of study: *Photography*

Known for: *Founding the Kodak company; inventing roll film*

Nationality: *American*

Birthplace: *Waterville, New York*

Date of birth: *July 12, 1854*

Date of death: *March 14, 1932*

Awards and honors: *George Eastman Award for Distinguished Contribution to the Art of Film given in his honor; appeared on a postage stamp, 1954*

Thomas Edison

Field of study: *Physics*

Known for: *Long-lasting lightbulb and many inventions*

Nationality: *American*

Birthplace: *Milan, Ohio*

Date of birth: *February 11, 1847*

Date of death: *October 18, 1931*

Awards and honors: *French Legion of Honor; awards from many other nations*

Albert Einstein

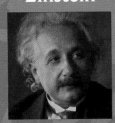

Field of study: *Physics*

Known for: *His theory of relativity ($E=mc^2$)*

Nationality: *German; German-Swiss; renounced German citizenship and became an American citizen*

Birthplace: *Ulm, Württemburg, Germany*

Date of birth: *March 14, 1879*

Date of death: *April 18, 1955*

Awards and honors: *Honorary doctorates in science, medicine, and philosophy; Nobel Prize in physics, 1921; Copley Medal awarded by Royal Society of London, 1925; Max Planck Medal, 1929*

Lawrence J. Fogel

Field of study: *Engineering*

Known for: *Inventing the noise canceling system*

Nationality: *American*

Birthplace: *Brooklyn, New York*

Date of birth: *March 2, 1928*

Date of death: *February 18, 2007*

Awards and honors: *Special assistant to the associate director at the National Science Foundation, 1960–1961; lifetime achievement award from the Evolutionary Programming Society, 1996; inaugeral IEEE Frank Rosenblatt Technical Field Award, 2006*

Elsa Garmire

Field of study: *Physics*

Known for: *Work in laser technology and optics*

Nationality: *American*

Birthplace: *Buffalo, New York*

Date of birth: *November 11, 1939*

Awards and honors: *Fellow, Optical Society of America, 1981; fellow, American Physical Society, 1996; national associate of the National Academies, 2004*

31

Alexander Graham Bell

Field of study: *Engineering*

Known for: *Inventing the telephone*

Nationality: *Scottish*

Birthplace: *Edinburgh, Scotland*

Date of birth: *March 3, 1847*

Date of death: *August 2, 1922*

Awards and honors: *Volta Prize, 1880; founding member of the National Geographic Society, 1888; second president of Society, 1897–1904; Regent of the Smithsonian Institution, 1898–1922; Albert Medal from the Royal Society of Arts, 1902; AIEE's Edison Medal, 1914; Alexander Graham Bell Institute, Gardens, Memorial Park, and Museum named for him; Bell Telephone Memorial erected in his honor*

Francesco Grimaldi

Fields of study: *Physics, mathematics*

Known for: *Suggesting that light travels in waves*

Nationality: *Italian*

Birthplace: *Bologna, Italy*

Date of birth: *April 2, 1618*

Date of death: *December 28, 1663*

Awards and honors: *Crater on the moon named for him*

Lene Vestergaard Hau

Field of study: *Physics*

Known for: *Slowing the speed of light*

Nationality: *Danish-American*

Birthplace: *Vejle, Denmark*

Date of birth: *November 13, 1959*

Awards and honors: *MacArthur Fellow, 2001-2006; NKT Award from the University of Copenhagen, 2001; appointed to the Royal Danish Academy of Sciences, 2002; fellow of American Academy of Arts and Sciences, 2009*

Kristina Johnson

Field of study: *Physics*

Known for: *Discovering new ways to create miniature lights for displays and computer monitors*

Nationality: *American*

Birthplace: *Colorado*

Year of birth: *1958*

Awards and honors: *First woman to become dean of the Pratt School of Engineering, 1999; Achievement Award from the Society of Women Engineers, 2004; John Fritz Medal from the American Association of Engineering Societies, 2008*

James Clerk Maxwell

Field of study: *Physics*

Known for: *Discovering that light is a form of electromagnetism and that it travels in waves*

Nationality: *British/Scottish*

Birthplace: *Edinburgh, Scotland*

Date of birth: *June 13, 1831*

Date of death: *November 5, 1879*

Awards and honors: *Mountain range on Venus, gap in the rings of Saturn, James Clerk Maxwell Telescope, building at University of Edinburgh, building at King's College, centre at Edinburgh Academy named for him*

Albert Abraham Michelson

Field of study: *Physics*

Known for: *Creating instruments to correctly measure light*

Nationality: *American*

Birthplace: *Strzelno, Prussia*

Date of birth: *December 19, 1852*

Date of death: *May 9, 1931*

Awards and honors: *Rumford Prize, 1888; Copley Medal, 1907; Nobel Prize in physics, 1907; first American to win Nobel Prize in sciences; Gold Medal from the Royal Astronomical Society, 1923*

Isaac Newton

Fields of study: *Physics, mathematics*

Known for: *Newton's laws of motion*

Nationality: *English*

Birthplace: *Woolsthorpe-by-Colsterworth, Lincolnshire, England*

Date of birth: *December 25, 1642*

Date of death: *March 20, 1727*

Awards and honors: *President of the Royal Society, knighted by Queen Ann*

Oberlin Smith

Field of study: *Engineering*

Known for: *Working with magnetic recording*

Nationality: *American*

Birthplace: *Cincinnati, Ohio*

Date of birth: *March 22, 1840*

Date of death: *July 19, 1926*

Awards and honors: *President of the American Society of Mechanical Engineers, 1899*

Jan Talbot

Field of study: *Chemical engineering*

Known for: *Work on nanoengineering*

Nationality: *American*

Birthplace: *Yokohama, Japan*

Date of birth: *December 24, 1952*

Awards and honors: *President of the Electrochemical Society, 2001–2002; fellow of the Electrochemical Society, 2004*

Thomas Young

Fields of study: *Physics, optics*

Known for: *Proposing that the color of light relates to wavelength*

Nationality: *British*

Birthplace: *Somerset, England*

Date of birth: *June 13, 1773*

Date of death: *May 10, 1829*

Awards and honors: *Young Medal given in his honor*

Light and Sound Through Time

c. 700 B.C.	Pythagoras incorrectly explains vision by saying rays go from the eye to an object; he also experiments with vibrating strings used to make music
c. 1030s A.D.	Arab scientist Haytham explains vision correctly by saying light rays reflect from objects and enter the eye
early 1600s	Italian scientist Galileo Galilei tries without success to measure the speed of light; he also studies vibrations and sound pitch and frequency
mid 1600s	French scientist Pierre Gassendi makes the first recorded attempt to measure the speed of sound in air
1666	English scientist Sir Isaac Newton discovers that white light contains all colors and that they can be separated using a prism
c. 1675	Danish astronomer Olaus Roemer proves that the speed of light has a limit
1678	Dutch physicist and astronomer Christiaan Huygens proposes that light moves in the form of waves
1826	Swiss physicist Daniel Colladon makes the first measurement of the speed of sound in water
1842	Austrian physicist Christian Doppler shows that sound waves from a source moving toward the listener seem to rise in frequency, and lower when the source is going away; this is known as the Doppler effect

1864	British physicist James Clerk Maxwell discovers that light is related to electricity and magnetism
1877	American inventor Thomas Edison creates the phonograph, the first device that can record and reproduce sounds
1878	British physicist Lord Rayleigh describes important principles of acoustics, the study of sound properties
1926	American physicist Albert Michelson accurately measures the speed of light
1947	American pilot Chuck Yeager becomes the first person to break the sound barrier
1953	American pilot Jacqueline Cochran becomes the first woman to break the sound barrier
1982	Compact discs that can store sound are sold for the first time, in Europe and Japan; they appear in the United States in 1983
1990	The Hubble Space Telescope, designed to peer deep into space using optical and infrared observation equipment, is placed in orbit; it eventually showed the formation of galaxies soon after the explosive birth of the universe
2008	American scientists Martin Chalfie and Robert Tsien and Japanese scientist Osamu Shimomura win the Nobel Prize in chemistry for isolating the protein in jellyfish that glows green when exposed to ultraviolet light
2009	U.S. astronauts make the last of several repair visits to the Hubble Space Telescope, which is expected to function until 2014

camera obscura—darkened chamber in which the real image of an object is received through a small opening or lens and focused in natural color onto a facing surface rather than recorded on a film or plate

electromagnetic—the interaction between electric and magnetic fields

frequency—rate at which an event occurs; for example, the number of wavelengths, or wave crests, that pass by a fixed point each second

gravity—force of attraction between two objects

matter—particles of which everything in the universe is made

microscope—device that uses lenses to magnify very small objects for scientific study

nanotechnology—any technology using tiny machines or devices, sometimes the size of a few atoms

optics—study of light

patent—the right to be the only one to make, use, or sell an invention for a certain number of years

physics—study of matter, energy, force, and motion

pitch—property of a sound determined by the frequency of the waves producing it

plague—disease that spreads rapidly

reflect—to bounce off the surface of an object

refract—change direction of light or sound waves as a result of entering a new medium

sonar—device that measures the distance to an object by bouncing sound waves off the object and timing how long it takes the waves to return

telescope—instrument made of lenses and mirrors that is used to view distant objects

Burgan, Michael. *Thomas Alva Edison: Great American Inventor*. Minneapolis: Compass Point Books, 2007.

Cook, Trevor. *Experiments with Light and Sound*. New York: PowerKidsPress, 2009.

Solway, Andrew. *Exploring Sound, Light, and Radiation*. New York: Rosen Central, 2008.

Stille, Darlene R. *Waves: Energy on the Move*. Minneapolis: Compass Point Books, 2006.

Wishinsky, Frieda. *Albert Einstein*. New York: DK Publishing, 2005.

Internet Sites

FactHound offers a safe, fun way to find Internet sites related to this book. All of the sites on FactHound have been researched by our staff.

Here's all you do:

Visit *www.facthound.com*

FactHound will fetch the best sites for you!

Index

Connie Jankowski

Connie Jankowski is a seasoned journalist, marketing expert, public relations consultant, and teacher. Her education includes a bachelor of arts from the University of Pittsburgh and graduate study at Pitt. She has worked in publishing, public relations, and marketing for the past 25 years. She is the author of 11 books and hundreds of magazine articles.

Image Credits